The Ruby Princess Runs Away

THE JEWEL KINGDOM

The Ruby Princess Runs Away

JAHNNA N. MALCOLM

Illustrations by Neal McPheeters

ISBN 0-590-21283-4

Text copyright © 1997 by Jahnna Beecham and Malcolm Hillgartner.
All rights reserved. Published by Scholastic Inc.
LITTLE APPLE PAPERBACKS is a trademark of Scholastic Inc.

12 11 10 9 8 7 6 5 4 3 2 1   8 9/9 0 1 2/0

Printed in the U.S.A.   40
First Scholastic printing, June 1997

Designed by Elizabeth B. Parisi

For Dash and Skye
The Shining Jewels in Our Lives

CONTENTS

———◆◆◆———

The Ruby Princess Runs Away

The Jewel Kingdom

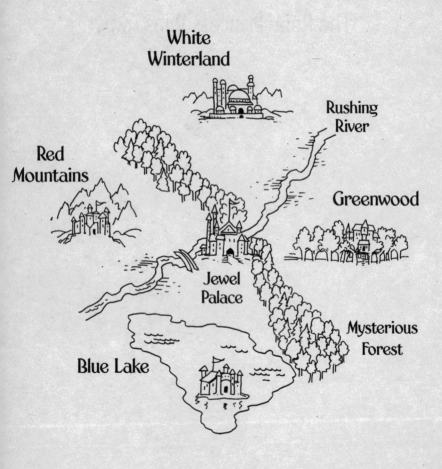

White
Winterland

Rushing
River

Red
Mountains

Greenwood

Jewel
Palace

Mysterious
Forest

Blue Lake

Roxanne Runs Away

 "I can't do it," Roxanne whispered from her hiding place in the royalberry tree. "I can't be a Jewel Princess. I'm not ready."

Today was the day she and her sisters would be crowned.

It was also the day they would leave the Jewel Palace where they had grown up.

As the Ruby Princess, Roxanne would have to move to her new castle in the Red Mountains. The mountains lay in the farthest corner of the Jewel Kingdom.

"I always knew this day would come," she murmured. "I just didn't think it would come so soon."

Roxanne stared glumly down at the palace courtyard. Creatures from every land were gathering there.

Sprites with blue skin and green hair chatted with goat-footed Fauns. Richly dressed lords and ladies bowed to pointy-eared elves who rode on the shoulders of smiling giants.

"There you are!" A little red bird with a rainbow plume on its head fluttered onto the limb next to Roxanne. It was Twitter, the royal secretary.

"The king and queen have been

looking for you everywhere!" Twitter squawked.

Queen Jemma and King Regal ruled the Jewel Kingdom. Today they were giving four of the Kingdom's lands to their daughters.

"Don't tell my parents where I am, Twitter," Roxanne pleaded. "I can't face them. Not yet."

"The ceremony is about to begin." Twitter tapped Roxanne's hand with his long yellow beak. "Everybody from the Jewel Kingdom is here."

Roxanne's big brown eyes widened. "Everybody?"

"Everybody who's anybody." Twitter ticked off the names of the guests on one wing. "There are the Gnomes, the Craghoppers, and the Pixies from the Red Mountains."

Roxanne gulped.

"Then there are all those creatures from the Greenwood, the Blue Lake, and the White Wonderland."

Those were her sisters' lands.

"Then there are your cousins — "

"Stop!" Roxanne pinched Twitter's beak closed. "If you're trying to make me nervous," she whispered, "you are doing a very good job."

Twitter shook his beak free from her grasp. He hopped to the limb above Roxanne's head.

"You shouldn't be nervous," Twitter said. "You should be excited, like your sisters."

Roxanne's youngest sister Emily had been up since dawn, chattering about being crowned the Emerald Princess.

Demetra, the Diamond Princess, was

the oldest of the four girls. She had spent the entire week in front of her mirror nervously weaving ribbons into her long brown hair.

Sabrina, the Sapphire Princess, was usually the quietest of the four. But even she had rattled on about Nymphs and Striders and all of the new friends she would make at the Blue Lake.

Every princess but Roxanne was happy.

"I just don't feel like a princess," she said with a huge sigh. "In fact, I feel very ordinary."

"Hush, my lady!" Twitter glanced nervously at the palace windows. "Someone might hear you."

"But Twitter, look at me." Roxanne stood up in the crook of the tree. "I'm just a regular girl. I'm ten years old. I like to climb trees, ride horses, and go swimming."

"That will change," Twitter murmured.

"I don't like dresses." Roxanne gestured to her beautiful, red velvet gown. "I'd rather wear breeches."

Twitter winced. "Heaven forbid."

"And how can I rule and protect the people of the Red Mountains, when I can't protect myself?"

Roxanne showed Twitter her leg. Her stockings were torn. And a very large lump had formed on her shin. "I banged my knee on the palace wall when I climbed up here."

Twitter fluttered in circles around the tree. "Oh, dear, oh, dear!"

Roxanne cocked her head. "How does a person rule, anyway?"

"How should I know?" Twitter ruffled his feathers. "You just order people around."

"Order people around." Roxanne wrinkled her nose. "That doesn't sound like fun."

"Who said being a princess was fun?" Twitter squawked.

Ta-ra ta-ra ta-ra!

The trumpets sounded at the front gate. The palace herald announced, "Presenting the magnificent wizard Gallivant!"

"Gallivant!" Roxanne gasped, nearly falling out of the tree.

The wizard was very old and very powerful. Just hearing his name made Roxanne weak in the knees.

"There he is." Below her, Roxanne could see the big white plumes of the horses that pulled the wizard's gleaming glass coach.

Twitter flew to a ledge in the courtyard to get a closer look. He called to the princess, "Gallivant is carrying the Great Jewelled Crown!"

The crown held the jewels of the kingdom. It was written that whoever possessed these jewels would rule the land.

Roxanne watched everyone in the courtyard bow low as the wizard passed.

"Soon they'll be bowing to me," Roxanne murmured. "I'll be in a coach with the Ruby Crown on my head. The coach will take me far away from my parents and my sisters. And there I'll sit all by myself in some lonely old castle . . ."

Roxanne's voice trailed off. The palace gates were standing wide open.

Her eyes widened. *I don't have to be*

crowned today, she thought. *I could just leap out of this tree and run away.*

Twitter flew back to her. "Hurry, my lady. You must join the king and queen and your sisters. They're about to greet the wizard."

Ta-ra ta-ra ta-ra!

The trumpets sounded again.

"It's now or never," Roxanne murmured, keeping her eyes fixed upon the open gate.

Queen Jemma and King Regal stepped onto the marble steps of the palace. A cheer rang from every creature in the courtyard.

Roxanne gathered her skirts around her, took a deep breath, and leaped. "Now!"

Strangers on the Road

"Princess, stop!" Twitter cried. He flapped his wings, trying to keep up with Roxanne as she raced down the mountain "You must come back to the palace!"

Roxanne ignored Twitter. She was too busy trying to run and put on her cape. She had grabbed the cape from one of the ladies-in-waiting as she raced through the palace gates.

"If you won't come back, then I'm coming with you!" Twitter declared, flying in front of her.

"Suit yourself," Roxanne huffed. "But I want you to know I won't be going back. I'm through with being a princess."

"Do you know where you're going?" Twitter asked. "I mean, after all, you've never been far from the palace before."

Twitter was right. Roxanne had only left the grounds twice. Once, when she was a baby, traveling to Gallivant's Cave. And another time on a butterfly-watching trip with Queen Jemma.

"I've seen maps!" Roxanne declared. She pointed to a glistening ribbon of water that ran across the fields in front of them. "I know that's the Rushing River."

"It moves very fast and is often difficult to cross," Twitter said.

Roxanne pointed to a gloomy stand of trees. It crept across the pastures like a big dark shadow. "That is the Mysterious Forest."

"Oooh." Twitter shuddered. "You want to stay away from there."

"Why?" Roxanne asked. "I've always been warned to keep away from the Mysterious Forest but no one has ever told me why."

"Because . . ." Twitter landed on her shoulder and whispered into her ear. "Because there is a secret passage in there. It leads straight to Castle Dread."

Roxanne's eyes widened. "Across the Black Sea? Where Lord Bleak and the evil Darklings were sent?"

Twitter nodded.

Roxanne had often heard terrible stories of Lord Bleak. He had once ruled the Jewel Kingdom. But that was in the Dark Times, before Roxanne was born.

"Then I don't think we really need to go in the Mysterious Forest," she said in a shaky voice. "I say we head west."

"West is good," Twitter said, glancing nervously back toward the dark woods. "The Red Mountains lie to the west."

Roxanne walked toward the Rushing River. "There should be a stone bridge just over that rise. I remember it from the maps in Father's study. We can cross the river there."

But as they reached the bridge, two figures in hooded black capes suddenly emerged from beneath it. They carried stout walking sticks and their hoods covered their faces.

"Where are you going my pretty?" one of them asked in a crackly voice.

A chill ran down Roxanne's spine. She pulled her cape shut to hide her fancy red dress.

"That's really none of your business!" Twitter squawked from his perch on her shoulder.

"What an unusual creature," the other cloaked figure rasped. It stretched one bony finger toward Twitter. "The rainbow plume. Aren't those the palace colors?"

"Yes," Roxanne said quickly. "We're on our way to the coronation."

"Oh, really?" The other stranger hobbled forward. "But the palace is behind you."

"My lady." Twitter pecked at Roxanne's shoulder. "My *lady*!"

She raised her hand to swat at the bird. "Twitter, please stop that!"

The hooded figures gasped. Roxanne realized they were staring at her gown.

One hissed to the other, "The Ruby Princess!"

Twitter tugged Roxanne away from them. "Th-th-these strangers," the bird stammered. "I think they may be D-d-dark — *awk!*"

His voice was cut off as a third stranger appeared from the woods and grabbed him.

"You let go of that bird!" Roxanne ordered.

"Come and get him," the figure whispered.

"Run, my lady!" Twitter coughed. "Run!"

Before Roxanne could make a move, a

black shadow darkened the sky above them.

Roxanne looked up.

A huge green creature with red scaly wings swooped toward her. It was breathing fire.

"By the Great Jewelled Crown," Roxanne cried, as the creature plucked her off the ground with its claws. "A dragon!"

Hapgood the Dragon

———— ❖ ————

 "Permit me to introduce myself," the dragon said when they were far away from the hooded creatures. He gently placed Roxanne on the ground. "My name is Hapgood."

Roxanne was still a little rattled from her quick flight through the air. "Hapgood?"

The big green dragon nodded. He

tucked his wings into his body and blinked his enormous dark blue eyes.

"But you may call me Happy," he said in a very deep, very formal voice.

"My name is — " Roxanne's hand flew to her mouth. She couldn't tell this dragon who she really was. Roxanne the runaway princess.

But she didn't want to lie to him, either. After all, he'd just rescued her from the hooded strangers. So she said, "I am Roxanne. Of the Rushing River."

The dragon held out one claw. She shook it — carefully.

"Pleased to meet you, Roxanne," Hapgood said. Then he added, "Of the Rushing River."

Roxanne couldn't help staring at the marvelous creature.

"I've only met one dragon before," she explained. "He was very fierce and spent a lot of time breathing fire. He burned up trees and chairs — anything made of wood. Are you fierce?"

The corners of Hapgood's mouth turned up in a smile. "I can be fierce when I want to be. But only when I meet creatures I don't like."

Roxanne looked back toward the bridge where the hooded strangers had tried to grab her. "I didn't like them one bit."

Hapgood's smile vanished and his eyes glowed red. "Those were Darklings. From Castle Dread. It's an ill sign when they appear in our kingdom."

"I wonder if Father — I mean, the king — knows about them," Roxanne murmured.

"My lady!" Twitter squawked from above them.

The little red bird was out of breath. His feathers were ruffled. One of his rainbow plumes was bent.

He fluttered onto a limb beside Roxanne's head. "I thought you'd been kidnapped!"

"No, Twitter!" Roxanne laughed. "I'm quite safe. Meet Hapgood."

Twitter turned up his beak at the big green dragon. "We've met," he sniffed. "He nearly burned off half my feathers with that flame of his."

Hapgood bowed his head. "Please accept my apologies. I was aiming for the Darklings."

Twitter's little black eyes widened. "I knew they were Darklings. Oh, this is not good. Not good at all."

Suddenly the ground beneath them began to tremble. The sound of hoofbeats filled the air.

Roxanne looked up to see a man wearing the rainbow colors of the Jewel Palace galloping toward them.

"It's Armoral, captain of the palace guards!" Roxanne cried.

He'll recognize me for sure, she thought.

"Hide me!" she pleaded, darting behind the dragon.

"Why? What have you done?" Hapgood asked.

Roxanne bit her lip, trying to think of something. "I, um . . . er, I . . ."

"She stole a banner from the palace courtyard," Twitter cut in. "She wanted a souvenir of the coronation."

Hapgood pulled a red and silver shield from under his wing. "Put this on your arm. It will make you and anyone you touch invisible."

Roxanne didn't ask any questions. She quickly strapped the shield to her arm. Then Twitter hopped onto her shoulder.

Hapgood whispered the magic words. *"Magic shield with power so bright, hide them from all others' sight."*

Roxanne and Twitter disappeared from view.

"You there, dragon!" Armoral called, pulling his horse to a stop. "The Ruby Princess has disappeared from the palace grounds. She was dressed all in red. Have you seen her pass this way?"

Roxanne squeezed her eyes shut tight. *Did Hapgood see my dress?* she wondered. *If he did, he'll know I'm the Ruby Princess.*

"No one has passed by me," Hapgood

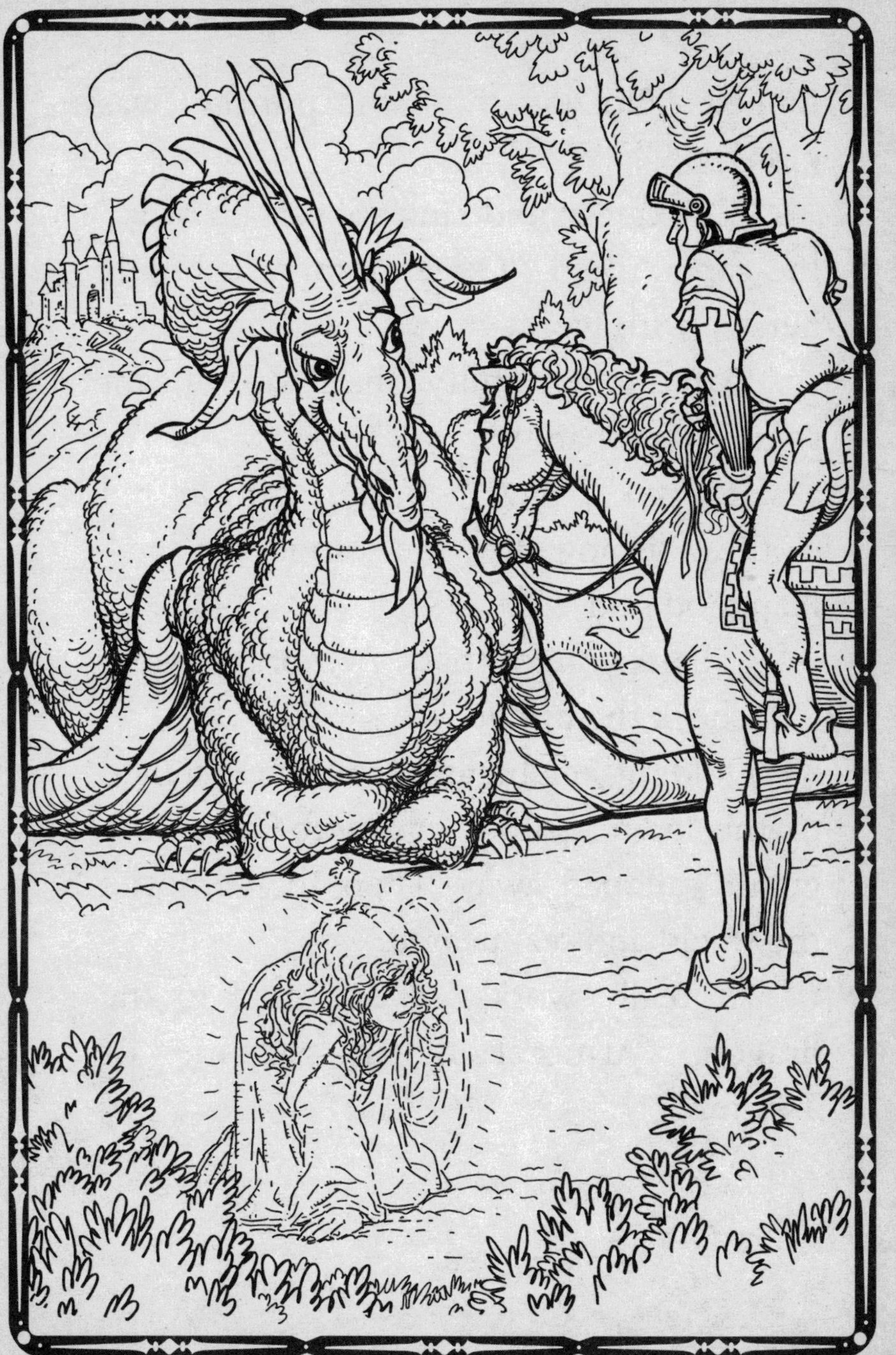

replied. "Do you think the princess was kidnapped?"

"The queen and king are certain of it," the captain said. "Queen Jemma is beside herself with worry."

Roxanne felt guilty. She hadn't meant to upset her parents.

"I think I saw a young girl in red clothes fishing by the stone bridge," Hapgood said.

"Thank you for that," Armoral barked. "I'll check the bridge."

Holding her breath, Roxanne listened to the fading sound of hoofbeats as the guard galloped away. Then she removed the shield and reappeared.

"It really works," she gasped to the dragon. "Armoral didn't see me or Twitter."

"No, he didn't," Hapgood replied. "But it wouldn't have mattered. He was looking for the Ruby Princess. And you aren't the Ruby Princess." He put his face right up to hers. "*Are* you?"

Roxanne swallowed hard. "No. I have not been crowned the Ruby Princess," she declared straight to Hapgood's face. "I am Roxanne of the Running River."

"Didn't you say, *Rushing* River?" Hapgood asked, raising one eyebrow.

"I mean, the Rushing River," Roxanne said quickly. "I'm just a little nervous right now."

"Well, the captain has gone to look for the princess at the river's edge," Twitter pointed out. "You needn't worry about him."

"Hopefully he'll see the Darklings and

tell the king about them," Roxanne murmured to Twitter.

She handed the magic shield back to Hapgood. "Thank you for the use of this wonderful shield."

Hapgood held up one claw. "Keep it. You may need it again. Remember, it has the power to make you invisible — but only for a short time."

"Someone's coming!" Twitter squawked. "Put on the shield."

Roxanne spun around as two squat figures hobbled toward them.

One was a little woman with fuzzy red hair and a round face. The other was a tiny man with a long gray beard. He was limping.

"Are they Darklings?" Roxanne asked Hapgood.

The dragon shook his head. "These are Gnomish folk from the Red Mountains."

Roxanne's eyes widened. That was to be her new home. "The Red Mountains?"

"Yes." Hapgood frowned. "And they appear to be in trouble!"

4

Applesap and Marigold

 "My name is Applesap," the little, bearded Gnome said. "And this is my wife, Marigold."

"We need help," Marigold cried. "We've been attacked."

"You're hurt!" Roxanne cried, kneeling beside the little man. "Your leg has a terrible gash on it."

Roxanne tore a strip of white cotton

from her petticoat and handed it to Twitter. "Take this to the Rushing River. Dip it in the water and hurry back."

"Right away!" Twitter flapped off as fast as his wings would carry him.

Marigold had a scarf tied over her flaming-red hair. Her cheeks were dirty and streaked with tears.

"They came out of nowhere," she cried, burying her face in her hands. "And took everything we had."

"Who did this?" Hapgood boomed.

"Darklings," Applesap moaned.

"They're terrible creatures," Marigold said with a shiver. "Just terrible." She put her arm around her husband's shoulder and cried, "Poor Applesap."

Roxanne frowned. "Does your leg hurt much?"

"It's not my leg," Applesap said, slumping down on a rock by the side of the road.

"It's his heart," Marigold murmured. "It's broken."

"You see, I'm a goldsmith," Applesap explained. "I was given the great honor of forging the crown for the Princess of the Red Mountains."

"The Ruby Princess?" Twitter asked, as he returned with the wet cloth.

Applesap nodded miserably. "I was bringing it to the great wizard Gallivant. He was to place the Ruby in it and crown our princess."

Roxanne's heart went out to the little Gnome. "Dear Mr. Applesap," she said, as she gently cleaned his wound with the wet cloth. "You can make another crown, just as fine as the first one."

"And I can fly you to the Jewel Palace," Hapgood offered.

"But I can't go to the palace empty-handed," Applesap said. "What would the princess think?"

"She would think you were a very sweet man who's had an awful experience," Roxanne replied. "And she would invite you to have a nice cup of wildroot tea with her."

Applesap laughed. "I wish."

"But you don't have to worry about that," Twitter cut in. "The princess has disappeared. Run away."

Marigold shook her head. "That's not true. We saw the princess crossing Buttercup Meadow."

"What?!" Roxanne and Twitter gasped.

"Marigold's right," Applesap said. "The princess was traveling in a beautiful glass coach. She was dressed all in red."

Marigold pointed to the hem of Roxanne's dress peeking out from under her cloak. "Like your dress there, miss."

Roxanne leaped to her feet. "Are you sure about this?"

"Cross my heart," Marigold said.

"I even heard a knight in black armor cry, 'Make way for the Ruby Princess!' " Applesap said.

Roxanne turned to Hapgood. "We have to go to the palace at once."

"But why?" Hapgood asked.

Roxanne tilted her chin high and declared, "Because that princess is an imposter!"

Imposter on the Throne!

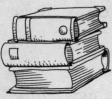Roxanne stared at the dragon and the two little Gnomes. None of them had moved a muscle.

"Didn't you hear what I said?" she repeated. "That princess is not a real princess."

"How — how do *you* know that?" Marigold asked.

"Because . . . because . . ." Roxanne turned to Twitter for help.

"Because this lady is a friend of the princess," Twitter explained quickly.

"That's right." Roxanne nodded. "We're the best of friends."

"And," Twitter continued, "she *knows* that the princess ran away."

Applesap squinted one eye shut. "But why would the princess want to run away?"

Roxanne took a deep breath. "You see . . . the princess told me she doesn't feel ready to rule a whole land. She doesn't know how."

Marigold and Applesap looked at each other and back at Roxanne.

"But I thought she was trained for that sort of thing," Applesap said.

"She was." Roxanne tore another strip of cloth from her petticoat as she explained, "The princess had her own tutor. They studied the Great Books telling of the Dark Times."

"Ah, yes." Hapgood nodded. "When Lord Bleak and the Darklings ruled our kingdom."

Roxanne tied the bandage around Applesap's leg. "The princess learned geography, too. She studied the kingdom's lands and the creatures that live in them."

"Did she learn to dance?" Marigold asked. "I love dancing."

"Oh, yes!" Roxanne giggled. "And how to sing, too."

"How nice," Marigold nodded pleasantly.

"She learned how to bow and look

very regal," Roxanne finished. "But no one taught her how to rule."

Marigold shrugged. "If you ask me, ruling is very simple."

"All we ask is that our princess have a keen ear and a kind heart," Applesap said.

"So that she might hear our problems and help us solve them," Marigold added.

"That's all?" Roxanne asked. "That just sounds like a friend."

Marigold and Applesap smiled.

"That's right," Marigold said. "We would like the Ruby Princess to be our friend."

Roxanne looked confused. "But that's easy."

"For some," Hapgood observed. "But not for everyone."

Twitter fluttered anxiously overhead. "I hate to break up this tea party," he cut in.

"But someone *really* must go to the palace. We have to stop them from crowning the wrong princess."

"I'll go!" Hapgood cried, raising up on his hind legs. "And I'll take all of you with me. Hop on my back."

Marigold helped Applesap to his feet. The two Gnomes climbed carefully onto the dragon's shoulders.

Roxanne frowned. "There really isn't room for all four of us."

"Then I'll stay," Applesap declared. "And you go. My leg feels much better, thanks to you."

Roxanne was torn. She knew she should go to the palace immediately. But Applesap was hurt. They couldn't leave him on the road. What if the Darklings came back?

"Applesap, you're hurt," Roxanne

finally said. "You should ride. And Marigold, you should go with your husband. I can follow on foot."

"Then I'll travel with you," Twitter said, hopping off Hapgood's neck.

"I'll take Applesap and Marigold to the palace," the dragon said. "But how can we stop the coronation?"

"You don't need to stop it," Roxanne said. "Just delay it. I'll bring proof that she is a fake."

"We'll do our best." Hapgood unfolded his mighty red wings. "Be careful, Lady Roxanne of the Rushing River."

Roxanne placed one hand over her heart. "I'll be very careful."

With a swoosh, Hapgood rose into the air. "And if anything unpleasant happens, use the magic shield."

Roxanne waved at the two Gnomes

clinging to the dragon's neck. "I'll see you all at the Jewel Palace."

Hapgood wheeled in a circle and ordered, "Take the shortcut. You'll save time."

"Where is it?" Twitter called.

The dragon boomed a reply that Roxanne did not want to hear.

"Through the Mysterious Forest!"

The Mysterious Forest

Roxanne and Twitter followed a winding path deep into the Mysterious Forest. It was darker and colder than Roxanne had ever imagined.

"Twitter?" Roxanne whispered.

"Yes, my lady?" Twitter whispered back. He was riding on her shoulder.

"I'm scared."

"If it makes you feel any better," Twitter replied, "so am I. Look." He held up one red wing. "All of my feathers are shaking."

The trees in the forest were black and twisted. The bushes were covered with long thorns. The smell of rotting leaves hung in the air.

A thorny branch reached out and tore Roxanne's skirt.

"Help!" Roxanne squeaked. "That bush tried to grab me."

"I wish we'd taken the long route," Twitter muttered. "I don't like this place one bit. It feels evil."

"It is," Roxanne said with a gulp. "Hapgood says there is a path here that leads directly to Castle Dread. Across the Black Sea."

"I don't doubt it." Twitter pecked Roxanne on the top of the head. "Walk faster, would you?"

Roxanne tried to go faster. But every step was hard. Thick roots tripped her feet. Black vines dropped from above and pulled at her hair.

Suddenly she stopped dead still.

"What is it?" Twitter asked. "Why are we stopping?"

"Voices," Roxanne whispered. "I hear voices. Just around the blackthorn bush."

"I'll go see." Twitter left Roxanne's shoulder. He flew to the bend in the path.

All of Twitter's feathers stood on end. He opened his beak but no sound came out.

"What is it, Twitter?" Roxanne whispered, creeping up beside him.

"Those Darklings!" he croaked. "The three from the bridge. They're camped ahead. Turn back!"

"We can't, Twitter. We have to get to the palace."

"But the Darklings," Twitter peeped. "They'll stop us."

Roxanne remembered the shield Hapgood had given her. "Not if they can't see us."

"What do you mean?" Twitter asked with a puzzled look on his face.

Roxanne held up the shield and smiled. "We'll hide, Twitter. Hop on my shoulder. We'll be invisible."

Once Twitter was on her shoulder, Roxanne held the shield in front of her and murmured the words Hapgood had taught her:

Magic shield with power so bright,
Hide us from all others' sight.

"Now let's go," she whispered.

Twitter tapped her cheek. "Be careful, Princess."

Three Darklings in black capes were huddled around a map.

Roxanne started to tiptoe past, but something they said stopped her.

"Our plan is working perfectly," the leader said in a deep voice.

"Can you believe our good luck?" the shortest one snorted. "We were supposed to kidnap Princess Roxanne but she saved us the trouble by running away."

The third one laughed hoarsely. "With the real Roxanne out of the way, we can put our own princess on the throne."

"Our princess is already at the palace. I sent the carriage there myself," the shortest Darkling declared.

"Have you taken care of the shape-changing mask?" the leader asked.

"Yes. Princess Rudgrin is wearing it. She is now Roxanne's mirror image."

"Rudgrin?" Roxanne whispered to Twitter. "Isn't she the daughter of Lord Bleak? I thought they were banished from our kingdom forever."

"They were," Twitter replied. "All the Darklings were. But it looks like they're back."

"With Rudgrin securely on the throne in the Red Mountains," the Darkling leader said, "we can then replace the other princesses, one by one."

Roxanne's eyes widened. "They plan to take over the Jewel Kingdom!"

"Oh, dear! Oh, dear! We have to keep them from leaving the forest," Twitter fretted. "But how?"

Roxanne looked around the Darklings' campsite.

Two giant roothogs and a gray-winged Gorax were tied at the edge of the clearing. The roothogs were pulling up the roots of some blackthorn bushes with their tusks.

"I've got an idea," Roxanne said.

"What is it?"

"Those two roothogs and that Gorax must be their rides," Roxanne whispered. "If we can tie the bird and the hogs to each other, then we can stall the Darklings."

"And that will give us enough time to run to the palace for help," Twitter whispered.

"Exactly," Roxanne replied. "But we

better hurry. I don't know how long this shield will hide us."

Roxanne slipped as silently as she could through the thick brush, grabbing a rope from beside the Darklings.

She tied the first roothog's reins to the other roothog.

Then she made a large loop and swung that over the Gorax's head.

Grrawk! The bird shrieked as the rope tightened around its neck.

Roxanne froze.

"What was that?" The tallest Darkling spun to look at the bird.

For the first time, Roxanne got a glimpse of a Darkling's face.

It was hideous. His face was twisted in a permanent scowl. His eyes were two black holes. His teeth were short and pointed.

Roxanne shut her eyes, remembering what her tutor had told her about the Darklings. *They were once a handsome people. But the evil inside them was so strong, it warped their features. Now they are as ugly outside as they are inside.*

Roxanne shivered. What if these terrible creatures really did take over the Jewel Kingdom? They would make it a horrible place to live. And it would be all her fault!

"I won't let that happen!" she declared to herself.

"What's that?" the leader asked the other Darklings. "Did one of you speak?"

"It must have been the Gorax," the short Darkling replied. "She hasn't been the same since we crossed the Black Sea."

"Back to our plan," the leader said, rolling up the map. "With Rudgrin safely on the throne, there is only one thing left to do. Find the real Ruby Princess and take her back to Castle Dread."

"Never!" Roxanne blurted out.

The Darklings turned just as the shield's magic wore off.

"Well, look who's here!" the leader hissed. "We're in luck!"

"Twitter," Roxanne cried. "We're no longer invisible!"

"What do we do?" Twitter squawked.

"Run!"

7

Fly to the Palace!

"Seize her!"

Two Darklings lunged for Roxanne. She fell backward into the gray-winged Gorax.

"Twitter!" Roxanne cried. "I have an idea."

She leaped onto the Gorax and nudged its sides with her heels.

"Fly!" she ordered.

The Gorax croaked. With a heavy

flapping of its gray wings, it lifted her off the ground.

"Stop!" the Darklings shrieked, leaping onto the roothogs.

"The bird is tied to the roothogs," Twitter cried. "It's lifting them off the ground!"

"Higher!" Roxanne urged the Gorax. The great bird dragged the hogs and riders into the top branches of a tree.

"They're all tangled up!" Twitter reported with glee.

"Cut the rope!" Roxanne ordered. "Or we'll be pulled back down."

"Leave it to me!" With a sharp *rat-a-tat* of his beak, Twitter sliced the rope in two.

"Yes!" Roxanne cried as the Gorax flew out of the trees. She prodded the Gorax

with her heels and commanded, "To the palace!"

"Well done, my lady!" Twitter cheered as they swooped out of the Mysterious Forest and flew toward the palace.

Roxanne wanted to smile. But she couldn't.

"We can't celebrate yet, Twitter. We still have to stop Rudgrin!"

When they reached the palace gates, Roxanne saw two tiny figures waving frantically.

"It's Applesap and Marigold!" she shouted. "Down, Gorax!"

The beast obediently glided to a halt near the waiting Gnomes.

"Thank heavens you're here," Applesap cried, as he limped forward. "Marigold and I tried to delay the crowning but they wouldn't listen to us."

"We told them about the Darklings stealing our crown," Marigold wailed. "But they insisted they already had the crown."

"And they do!" Applesap said. "The one the Darklings stole from me."

"Where's Hapgood?" Roxanne asked.

"He went back to look for you," Marigold said.

Ta-ra ta-ra ta-ra!

"Trumpets!" Twitter gasped. "They signal the coronation of the princesses. Oh, no! We're too late!"

"Not if I have anything to say about it!" Roxanne leaped off the Gorax and dashed up the palace steps.

When she reached the throne room, Roxanne clasped the jeweled door handles with both hands and took a deep breath. "Here goes!"

She threw open the doors. The great

wizard Gallivant had already crowned Roxanne's three sisters. Now he was presenting the Ruby Crown to Princess Rudgrin.

Roxanne's velvet gown was torn. Her hair was tangled with blackthorns. But she knew who she was and announced it in a loud, clear voice.

"I am Princess Roxanne, the Ruby Princess of the Jewel Kingdom, ruler of the Red Mountains," she cried. "And I command you to *stop!*"

A Princess at Last

 The Emerald Princess, the Sapphire Princess, and the Diamond Princess turned and stared.

The guests of the court stared.

Even King Regal and Queen Jemma were staring.

First at Roxanne. Then at the girl who sat on the throne.

"They're identical!" Queen Jemma cried.

"That girl is an imposter!" Roxanne declared. "Her name is Rudgrin. She's the daughter of Lord Bleak from Castle Dread."

Princess Sabrina and Princess Emily gasped at the mention of the Darkling lord. Princess Demetra nearly fainted.

"If this is true, why does she look like my daughter?" King Regal demanded.

"Because Rudgrin is wearing a mask," Roxanne replied.

"Guards!" Rudgrin shrieked. "Arrest her." She pointed at Roxanne. "*She's* the imposter."

Roxanne put both hands on her hips. "*You* are a *liar*."

"Oh, dear," Queen Jemma cried.

"Whatever shall we do?" She turned to Rudgrin. "This Roxanne certainly *looks* like my daughter."

Then the queen faced Roxanne. "But this Roxanne, with the torn dress and messy hair, *acts* like my daughter."

Gallivant stepped forward. "There is only one way to find out who is the true Ruby Princess."

"How?" King Regal asked.

Gallivant fixed his stern gaze on Roxanne and Rudgrin. "Which of you bears the sign?"

"Sign?" Rudgrin repeated. "What sign?"

"The mark of the Jewel Princess," Gallivant boomed. "It is something every princess is born with."

Roxanne smiled first at her sisters and then at the wizard.

"I bear the mark," she said, stepping forward.

She raised her right arm and carefully turned back the cuff of her sleeve. There, for all the world to see, was a ruby teardrop on her wrist.

"The mark in the shape of her Ruby!" Gallivant declared. "She who bears the mark will wear the crown."

Then Emily, Demetra, and Sabrina raised their wrists. They, too, had a mark in the shape of their jewel.

Suddenly their crowns began to gleam.

"Look!" a lady-in-waiting gasped. "The jewels! They're glowing."

Twitter, who had been hiding behind Roxanne, fluttered to Rudgrin. "You fake! Take off your mask."

"Noooo!" howled Rudgrin, as Twitter peeled the mask off her face with his beak.

The court gasped when her twisted, ugly face was revealed.

In the blink of an eye, Rudgrin was whisked out of the throne room by the palace guards. And Roxanne was ushered to the king and queen.

"I am so sorry," Roxanne said, hugging her mother and father tightly. "I nearly ruined everything."

Queen Jemma smoothed Roxanne's hair. "We're just glad to know you're safe."

Roxanne took her place beside her sisters. Sabrina blew her a kiss. Demetra squeezed her hand. "Welcome back," Emily whispered.

Now it was time for Roxanne to be crowned.

King Regal nodded to Gallivant, who signaled the court musicians.

Beautiful music filled the air.

Gallivant turned to the crowd. "The people of the Red Mountains have chosen one of their own to place the Ruby Crown on Princess Roxanne's head. Will he please come forward?"

There was a loud flapping and the room was filled with smoke.

Gallivant announced, "May I present — "

"Happy!" Roxanne cried with glee. Ignoring all royal manners, she raced to greet her friend. "It's you!"

Hapgood folded his wings and bowed low. "Greetings, Princess Roxanne of the Red Mountains." He winked and added, "And the Rushing River."

Roxanne wrapped her arms around his neck and whispered, "You must have known who I was all along."

"Yes, my lady," Hapgood confessed,

sheepishly. "I did. When you ran away, Gallivant gave me the shield and sent me to find you."

Gallivant then presented the Ruby Crown to Hapgood. The dragon raised it above Roxanne's head.

"Wait!" Roxanne cried, stopping the ceremony. "I would like the man who forged this beautiful crown to be by my side." She searched the room for the bearded Gnome.

Applesap and Marigold stood at the back of the hall, looking very embarrassed.

"Come forward, friends," Roxanne cried. "And join the celebration."

Marigold, Applesap, and Twitter approached the throne.

Then Hapgood set the glittering Ruby Crown on Roxanne's head. "From this moment, I vow to be your friend and protector for all the days of my life."

Tears of joy shone in Roxanne's eyes. She hugged and kissed each one of her sisters.

Then the Ruby Princess turned to face the court. "As the ruler of the Red Mountains, I vow to have a keen ear and a kind heart, that I might always be a loving and giving . . . friend."